Rainbow Brite™
Saves Christmas

by Justin Spelvin
Illustrations by Kora Oliver

SCHOLASTIC INC.

New York   Toronto   London   Auckland   Sydney
Mexico City   New Delhi   Hong Kong   Buenos Aires

ISBN 0-439-65933-7

RAINBOW BRITE™ © 2004 Hallmark Licensing, Inc.
Used under license by Scholastic Inc. All rights reserved. Published by Scholastic Inc.
SCHOLASTIC and associated logos are trademarks and/or registered trademarks of Scholastic Inc.

12 11 10 9 8 7 6 5 4 3 2 1   4 5 6 7 8/0

Printed in Singapore
First printing, October 2004

There were only two days left before Christmas. Rainbow Brite, the Color Kids, and all of the Sprites in Rainbow Land were very busy decorating for Christmas Eve.

"I just love Christmas!" Rainbow Brite cheered, looking out at all the fun. "But doesn't it feel like something is missing?"

Just then Stormy swooped in and, with a stamp of Sky Dancer's hooves, a very cheery Christmas snow began to fall over Rainbow Land.

"SNOW!" cried Starlite. "Now it's perfect!"

"Christmas is the best!" added Twink.

But not *everybody* agreed.

"Christmastime . . . PHOOEY!" Murky grunted as he watched the festivities. "Why would anyone like that ridiculous holiday?"

"Maybe because of all the pretty colors," Lurky answered, "and the presents and the . . ."

"That's enough, snowball-brain!" grumbled Murky. "We *don't like* Christmas!"

"We don't?" asked Lurky, hiding his hat.

"Presents? *Bleh!* No one brings *us* presents. Christmas cheer? *Bleh!*" grumbled Murky. "All that color and singing and dancing? *Bleh!* Snow? It never snows at the Pits!"

"You're right, Murky. *Bleh* on Christmas," agreed Lurky.

But Murky wasn't listening anymore. He was too busy thinking over his perfectly awful plan to ruin Christmas in Rainbow Land.

"Just wait until tomorrow. There won't be *any* Christmas cheer left!" Murky laughed. His cackles grew louder and louder, until all of the Pits shook with his laughter.

The next morning the Color Kids awoke to a big surprise. There under the Christmas tree was a present for each of them.

"But it's only Christmas Eve," said Red Butler.

"I wonder who they are from," whispered Shy Violet.

"Let's open them and see!" Patty O'Green called out as she tore into the wrapping paper with glee.

"It's empty!" said Buddy Blue. But just then, gray, gloomy clouds rose up from each of their boxes.

Murky watched it all with a wicked grin on his face.
"It's working! It's working!" Murky scowled.
"Yippee! What's working?" asked Lurky.
"My plan, you nincompoop!" growled Murky. "Christmas is finished!"

The clouds grew and grew, raining gloom and doom down on everything they passed. All the beautiful Christmas colors, decorations, ornaments, and Star Sprinkles faded and turned a dismal gray.

"We have to do something!" shouted Canary Yellow to her friends.

But gray clouds had settled over each of their heads, dampening all their Christmas cheer.

"Why?" asked Red Butler.

"Yeah, who cares about Christmas?" asked Buddy Blue.

"Not me," said Canary Yellow as a cloud finally settled on top of her head.

Meanwhile, Rainbow Brite was just waking up. But as soon as she walked out of the Color Castle she spotted her present beneath the tree.

"Oh, look! An early Christmas present!" she called.

But before she could open it Twink snatched the gift away.

"Don't open that! It's a trap!" he warned.

That's when Rainbow Brite noticed everything was a miserable gray.

"Oh, no! Twink, we have to bring back all of the Christmas colors!" cried Rainbow Brite.

She quickly reached for some Star Sprinkles but there weren't any left! They'd used them all to decorate the tree.

"Twink!" Rainbow Brite called out. "The Sprites need to make more Star Sprinkles right away!"

"That's part of the problem," said Twink.

Not only were all the Color Kids giving up on Christmas, so were their Sprites. If no one was mining the color crystals that meant no more Star Sprinkles. Which meant no more color . . . and NO MORE CHRISTMAS!

"Come on! We need your Christmas spirit!" Rainbow Brite said.

But Murky's clouds were too powerful.

"Christmas is canceled," smirked a faded Red Butler.

"Good riddance," said a gloomy Patty O'Green.

And with that, the Color Kids walked off, hoping to forget all about Christmas.

Rainbow Brite, Starlite, and Twink were the only ones left who hadn't given up on Christmas.

"What if we can't fix everything in time?" asked a nervous Twink.

"We just have to," answered Rainbow Brite.

"Rainbow Land looks about as cheery as the Pits," Starlite pointed out.

"That's it!" cried Rainbow Brite. "This has to be the work of Murky and Lurky! Who else would hate Christmas this much?"

With no time to lose, Rainbow Brite, Starlite, and
Twink headed off toward Murky and Lurky's dreary
home.

"Maybe if we just ask him nicely to give our colors
back . . ." Rainbow Brite suggested. "I mean, it *is*
Christmas after all."

But as they approached the front door, the friends started to have their doubts.

"Do we really have to?" asked Twink, clutching Rainbow Brite's hand.

"This is the only way to save Christmas, Twink," Rainbow Brite reassured him.

She summoned her courage and knocked on the cold, dark, wooden door.

"You want me to W-W-WHAT?!?" Murky couldn't believe his ears!

"Give us back our colors, please," pleaded Rainbow Brite. "Don't you see? This is the season for joy and goodwill . . ."

". . . And b-b-being n-n-nice to others," added a shivering Twink.

"But I *hate* Christmas!" screamed Murky. "That's why I ruined it! You're never getting your colors back!"

"Never ever!" Lurky chimed in.

Rainbow Brite and Twink quickly realized that trying to reason with Murky wasn't going to get them anywhere. They slowly began backing up toward the door.

"Why shouldn't I ruin Christmas?!" Murky continued shouting.

"Do I get presents? NO! Do I get snow? NO! Does anyone ever wish me a Nasty Christmas? NO!"

Just as Rainbow Brite reached for the door, Murky cried out, "Cage 'em!"

Lurky sprang out with two cages, but then tripped over his own feet. As Rainbow Brite and Twink made it safely out of the house, Lurky only managed to catch one very cranky Murky.

"How did it go?" asked Starlite as they flew away from the Pits.

"It was a disaster," cried Twink. "Christmas is doomed."

"Maybe not," said Rainbow Brite. "Maybe Murky just needs a little Christmas cheer of his own."

A few hours later, Rainbow Brite, Starlite, and Twink returned to the Pits. With a quick knock on the door, Rainbow Brite deposited a little surprise for Murky on his doorstep, and then ran to hide with her friends.

"Who is that?" shouted Murky from inside. Then he opened the door just a little bit and snatched in the present.

KEEP OUT!

"What is *this*?" Murky asked, holding up the box, looking puzzled.

"Why, that looks just like a Christmas present," said Lurky.

"Don't be such a snowball-brain! No one gives *me* Christmas presents," snapped Murky.

"Look — there's a card," added Lurky.
Murky snorted before reading the card out loud,
"To Murky. We wish you a very Nasty Christmas."

No one had ever, ever thought to send Murky a Christmas present before. He shook it. He sniffed it. He listened to it. All the while a smile was creeping to his lips.

"Open it, Murky!" shouted Lurky.

That's just what he did. And from out of the box sprang the rays of rainbow joy, happiness, and Christmas goodwill that Rainbow Brite had carefully packed. The colors swirled all around Murky. They lifted him up. They brightened his spirits. They actually made him feel . . . happy!

Starlite, Twink, and Rainbow Brite could see all of the colors bursting out of the box.

"Look! It's working! It's working!" Rainbow Brite cheered.

And then they heard Murky say the most amazing words.

"MERRY CHRISTMAS!" he called. "MERRY CHRISTMAS!"

With that, a big, beautiful Christmas rainbow came shooting out from the Pits toward all of Rainbow Land.

The rainbow restored all the colors and shooed away every single gloomy cloud.

"What are we doing sitting around?" Red Butler shook his head.

"Yeah! It's Christmas Eve!" Canary Yellow called out.

"It's time for our party," cheered Patty O'Green.

The Color Kids and the Sprites quickly got right to work.

It was the best Christmas Eve party ever. There was singing, dancing, gift giving, and decorating. Everything was colorful and happy. And everyone was bursting with Christmas cheer.

"Merry Christmas, everyone!" Rainbow Brite called out.

"Merry, Merry Christmas," all of Rainbow Land answered.

Not so far away, there was another Christmas party going on — a little quieter, but no less merry. Murky and Lurky exchanged gifts for the first time ever. And Rainbow Brite asked Stormy to send them a beautiful snowfall. It was the very first white Christmas at the Pits.